The Medicine Wagon

This story tells children to be very careful about medicines, and that only their parents know what's good for them.

Story by:
Phil Baron

From treatment by:
Don Riedel

Illustrated by:
David High
Russell Hicks
Theresa Mazurek
Julie Armstrong
Allyn Conley/Gorniak

WORLDS OF WONDER™

D0573020

Grubby™ Newton Gimmick™ Princess Aruzia™ Leota™ Wooly What's-It™ Prince Arin™ Fobs™

"In My Medicine Wagon"

A medicine salesman rolled
up in an old wagon.

Just one swallow of my
magic potion will make
you handsome.

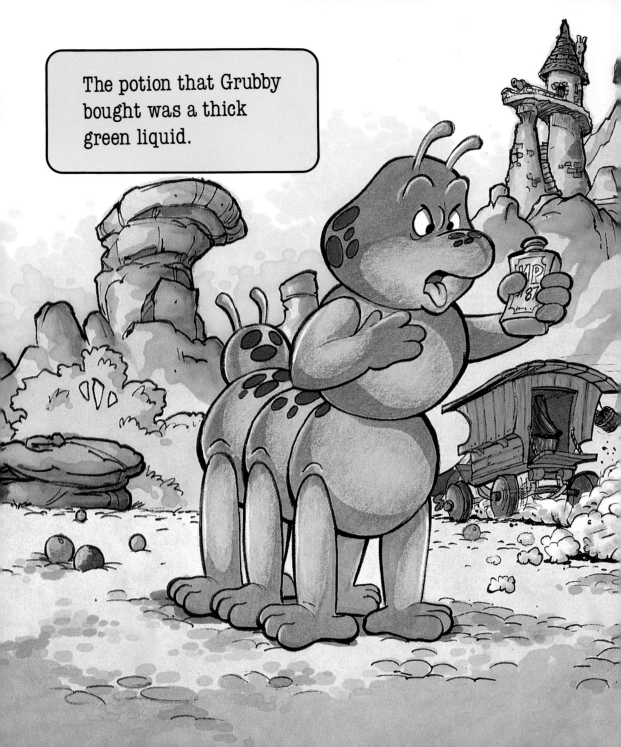

Little flowers and grass were popping up out of the paste on Gimmick's head.

We rushed Gimmick inside and away from the bees.

The gunk on Gimmick's head turned out to be nothing but dirt and water.

Your parents are the only ones who know what's good for you.